JEAN
RHYS

LET THEM CALL IT JAZZ
AND OTHER STORIES

PENGUIN BOOKS

PENGUIN BOOKS

Published by the Penguin Group. Penguin Books Ltd, 27 Wrights Lane, London w8 5TZ, England. Penguin Books USA Inc., 375 Hudson Street, New York, New York 10014, USA. Penguin Books Australia Ltd, Ringwood, Victoria, Australia. Penguin Books Canada Ltd, 10 Alcorn Avenue, Toronto, Ontario, Canada M4V 3B2. Penguin Books (NZ) Ltd, 182–190 Wairau Road, Auckland 10, New Zealand · Penguin Books Ltd, Registered Offices: Harmondsworth, Middlesex, England · 'Let Them Call It Jazz' and 'Outside the Machine' are taken from *Tigers are Better-Looking* and 'The Insect World' from *Sleep It Off Lady*, published by Penguin Books in 1973 and 1979 respectively. This edition published 1995 · Copyright © Jean Rhys, 1960, 1962, 1976. All rights reserved · Typeset by Datix International Limited, Bungay, Suffolk. Printed in England by Clays Ltd, St Ives plc · Except in the United States of America, this book is sold subject to the condition that it shall not, by way of trade or otherwise, be lent, re-sold, hired out, or otherwise circulated without the publisher's prior consent in any form of binding or cover other than that in which it is published and without a similar condition including this condition being imposed on the subsequent purchaser · 10 9 8 7 6 5 4 3 2 1

CONTENTS

Let Them Call It Jazz

One bright Sunday morning in July I have trouble
with my Notting Hill landlord because he ask for a
month's rent in advance. He tell me this after I live
there since winter, settling up every week without
fail. I have no job at the time, and if I give the
money he want there's not much left. So I refuse.
The man drunk already at that early hour, and he
abuse me – all talk, he can't frighten me. But his
wife is a bad one – now she walk in my room and say
she must have cash. When I tell her no, she give my
suitcase one kick and it burst open. My best dress
fall out, then she laugh and give another kick. She
say month in advance is usual, and if I can't pay find
somewhere else.

Don't talk to me about London. Plenty people
there have heart like stone. Any complaint – the
answer is 'prove it'. But if nobody see and bear
witness for me, how to prove anything? So I pack up
and leave. I think better not have dealings with that
woman. She too cunning, and Satan don't lie worse. 1

I walk about till a place nearby is open where I can have coffee and a sandwich. There I start talking to a man at my table. He talk to me already, I know him, but I don't know his name. After a while he ask, 'What's the matter? Anything wrong?' and when I tell him my trouble he say I can use an empty flat he own till I have time to look around.

This man is not at all like most English people. He see very quick, and he decide very quick. English people take long time to decide – you three-quarter dead before they make up their mind about you. Too besides, he speak very matter of fact, as if it's nothing. He speak as if he realize well what it is to live like I do – that's why I accept and go.

He tell me somebody occupy the flat till last week, so I find everything all right, and he tell me how to get there – three-quarters of an hour from Victoria Station, up a steep hill, turn left, and I can't mistake the house. He give me the keys and an envelope with a telephone number on the back. Underneath is written 'After 6 p.m. ask for Mr Sims'.

In the train that evening I think myself lucky, for to walk about London on a Sunday with nowhere to go – that take the heart out of you.

I find the place and the bedroom of the downstairs

flat is nicely furnished – two looking glass, wardrobe, chest of drawers, sheets, everything. It smell of jasmine scent, but it smell strong of damp too.

I open the door opposite and there's a table, a couple chairs, a gas stove and a cupboard, but this room so big it look empty. When I pull the blind up I notice the paper peeling off and mushrooms growing on the walls – you never see such a thing.

The bathroom the same, all the taps rusty. I leave the two other rooms and make up the bed. Then I listen, but I can't hear one sound. Nobody come in, nobody go out of that house. I lie awake for a long time, then I decide not to stay and in the morning I start to get ready quickly before I change my mind. I want to wear my best dress, but it's a funny thing – when I take up that dress and remember how my landlady kick it I cry. I cry and I can't stop. When I stop I feel tired to my bones, tired like old woman. I don't want to move again – I have to force myself. But in the end I get out in the passage and there's a postcard for me. 'Stay as long as you like. I'll be seeing you soon – Friday probably. Not to worry.' It isn't signed, but I don't feel so sad and I think, 'All right, I wait here till he come. Perhaps he know of a job for me.'

Nobody else live in the house but a couple on the top floor – quiet people and they don't trouble me. I have no word to say against them.

First time I meet the lady she's opening the front door and she give me a very inquisitive look. But next time she smile a bit and I smile back – once she talk to me. She tell me the house very old, hundred and fifty year old, and she and her husband live there since long time. 'Valuable property,' she says, 'it could have been saved, but nothing done of course.' Then she tells me that as to the present owner – if he is the owner – well he have to deal with local authorities and she believe they make difficulties. 'These people are determined to pull down all the lovely old houses – it's shameful.'

So I agree that many things shameful. But what to do? What to do? I say it have an elegant shape, it make the other houses in the street look cheap trash, and she seem pleased. That's true too. The house sad and out of place, especially at night. But it have style. The second floor shut up, and as for my flat, I go in the two empty rooms once, but never again.

Underneath was the cellar, full of old boards and broken-up furniture – I see a big rat there one day.

It was no place to be alone in I tell you, and I get

the habit of buying a bottle of wine most evenings, for I don't like whisky and the rum here no good. It don't even *taste* like rum. You wonder what they do to it.

After I drink a glass or two I can sing and when I sing all the misery goes from my heart. Sometimes I make up songs but next morning I forget them, so other times I sing the old ones like *Tantalizin'* or *Don't Trouble Me Now*.

I think I go but I don't go. Instead I wait for the evening and the wine and that's all. Everywhere else I live – well, it doesn't matter to me, but this house is different – empty and no noise and full of shadows, so that sometimes you ask yourself what make all those shadows in an empty room.

I eat in the kitchen, then I clean up everything and have a bath for coolness. Afterwards I lean my elbows on the windowsill and look at the garden. Red and blue flowers mix up with the weeds and there are five-six apple trees. But the fruit drop and lie in the grass, so sour nobody want it. At the back, near the wall, is a bigger tree – this garden certainly take up a lot of room, perhaps that's why they want to pull the place down.

Not much rain all the summer, but not much

sunshine either. More of a glare. The grass get brown and dry, the weeds grow tall, the leaves on the trees hang down. Only the red flowers – the poppies – stand up to that light, everything else look weary.

I don't trouble about money, but what with wine and shillings for the slot-meters, it go quickly; so I don't waste much on food. In the evening I walk outside – not by the apple trees but near the street – it's not so lonely.

There's no wall here and I can see the woman next door looking at me over the hedge. At first I say good evening, but she turn away her head, so afterwards I don't speak. A man is often with her, he wear a straw hat with a black ribbon and goldrim spectacles. His suit hang on him like it's too big. He's the husband it seems and he stare at me worse than his wife – he stare as if I'm wild animal let loose. Once I laugh in his face because why these people have to be like that? I don't bother them. In the end I get that I don't even give them one single glance. I have plenty other things to worry about.

To show you how I felt. I don't remember exactly. But I believe it's the second Saturday after I come
6 that when I'm at the window just before I go for

my wine I feel somebody's hand on my shoulder and it's Mr Sims. He must walk very quiet because I don't know a thing till he touch me.

He says hullo, then he tells me I've got terrible thin, do I ever eat. I say of course I eat but he goes on that it doesn't suit me at all to be so thin and he'll buy some food in the village. (That's the way he talk. There's no village here. You don't get away from London so quick.)

It don't seem to me he look very well himself, but I just say bring a drink instead, as I am not hungry.

He come back with three bottles – vermouth, gin and red wine. Then he ask if the little devil who was here last smash all the glasses and I tell him she smash some, I find the pieces. But not all. 'You fight with her, eh?'

He laugh, and he don't answer. He pour out the drinks then he says, 'Now, you eat up those sandwiches.'

Some men when they are there you don't worry so much. These sort of men you do all they tell you blindfold because they can take the trouble from your heart and make you think you're safe. It's nothing they say or do. It's a feeling they can give you. So I don't talk with him seriously – I don't want to spoil that evening. But I ask about the house and why it's so empty and he says:

'Has the old trout upstairs been gossiping?'

I tell him, 'She suppose they make difficulties for you.'

'It was a damn bad buy,' he says and talks about selling the lease or something. I don't listen much.

We were standing by the window then and the sun low. No more glare. He puts his hand over my eyes. 'Too big – much too big for your face,' he says and kisses me like you kiss a baby. When he takes his hand away I see he's looking out at the garden and he says this – 'It gets you. My God it does.'

I know very well it's not me he means, so I ask him, 'Why sell it then? If you like it, keep it.'

'Sell what?' he says. 'I'm not talking about this damned house.'

I ask what he's talking about. 'Money,' he says. 'Money. That's what I'm talking about. Ways of making it.'

'I don't think so much of money. It don't like me and what do I care?' I was joking, but he turns around, his face quite pale and he tells me I'm a fool. He tells me I'll get pushed around all my life and die like a dog, only worse because they'd finish off a dog, but they'll let me live till I'm a caricature of myself. That's what he say, 'Caricature of yourself.' He say I'll curse the day I was born and everything and everybody in this bloody world before I'm done.

I tell him, 'No I'll never feel like that,' and he smiles, if you can call it a smile, and says he's glad I'm content with my lot. 'I'm disappointed in you, Selina. I thought you had more spirit.'

'If I contented that's all right,' I answer him. 'I don't see very many looking contented over here.' We're standing staring at each other when the doorbell rings. 'That's a friend of mine,' he says. 'I'll let him in.'

As to the friend, he's all dressed up in stripe pants and a black jacket and he's carrying a briefcase. Very ordinary looking but with a soft kind of voice.

'Maurice, this is Selina Davis,' says Mr Sims, and Maurice smiles very kind but it don't mean much, then he looks at his watch and says they ought to be getting along.

At the door Mr Sims tells me he'll see me next week and I answer straight out, 'I won't be here next week because I want a job and I won't get one in this place.'

9

'Just what I'm going to talk about. Give it a week longer, Selina.'

I say, 'Perhaps I stay a few more days. Then I go. Perhaps I go before.'

'Oh no you won't go,' he says.

They walk to the gates quickly and drive off in a yellow car. Then I feel eyes on me and it's the woman and her husband in the next door garden watching. The man make some remark and she look at me so hateful, so hating I shut the front door quick.

I don't want more wine. I want to go to bed early because I must think. I must think about money. It's true I don't care for it. Even when somebody steal my savings – this happen soon after I get to the Notting Hill house – I forget it soon. About thirty pounds they steal. I keep it roll up in a pair of stockings, but I go to the drawer one day, and no money. In the end I have to tell the police. They ask me exact sum and I say I don't count it lately, about thirty pounds. 'You don't know how much?' they say. 'When did you count it last? Do you remember? Was it before you move or after?'

I get confuse, and I keep saying, 'I don't remem-ber,' though I remember well I see it two days before. They don't believe me and when a policeman come to the house I hear the landlady tell him, 'She certainly had no money when she came here. She wasn't able to pay a month's rent in advance for her room though it's a rule in this house.' 'These people terrible liars,' she say and I think 'It's you a terrible liar, because when I come you tell me weekly or monthly as you like.' It's from that time she don't speak to me and perhaps it's she take it. All I know is I never see one penny of my savings again, all I know is they pretend I never have any, but as it's gone, no use to cry about it. Then my mind goes to my father, for my father is a white man and I think a lot about him. If I could see him only once, for I too small to remember when he was there. My mother is fair coloured woman, fairer than I am they say, and she don't stay long with me either. She have a chance to go to Venezuela when I three-four year old and she never come back. She send money instead. It's my grandmother take care of me. She's quite dark and what we call 'country-cookie' but she's the best I know.

She save up all the money my mother send, she don't keep one penny for herself – that's how I get to England. I was a bit late in going to school regular, getting on for twelve years, but I can sew very beautiful, excellent – so I think I get a good job – in London perhaps.

However here they tell me all this fine handsewing take too long. Waste of time – too slow. They want somebody to work quick and to hell with the small stitches. Altogether it don't look so good for me, I must say, and I wish I could see my father. I have his name – Davis. But my grandmother tell me, 'Every word that comes out of that man's mouth a damn lie. He is certainly first class liar, though no class otherwise.' So perhaps I have not even his real name.

Last thing I see before I put the light out is the postcard on the dressing table. 'Not to worry.'

Not to worry! Next day is Sunday, and it's on the Monday the people next door complain about me to the police. That evening the woman is by the hedge, and when I pass her she says in very sweet quiet voice, '*Must* you stay? *Can't* you go?' I don't answer. I walk out in the street to get rid of her. But she run inside her house to the window, she can still see me. Then I start to sing, so she can understand I'm not afraid of her. The husband call out: 'If you don't stop that noise I'll send for the police.' I answer them quite short. I say, 'You go to hell and take your wife with you.' And I sing louder.

The police come pretty quick – two of them. Maybe they just round the corner. All I can say about police, and how they behave, is I think it all depends who they dealing with. Of my own free will I don't want to mix up with police. No.

One man says, you can't cause this disturbance here. But the other asks a lot of questions. What is my name? Am I tenant of a flat in No. 17? How long have I lived there? Last address and so on. I get vexed the way he speak and I tell him, 'I come here because somebody steal my savings. Why you don't look for my money instead of bawling at me? I work hard for my money. All-you don't do one single thing to find it.'

'What's she talking about?' the first one says, and the other one tells me, 'You can't make that noise here. Get along home. You've been drinking.'

I see that woman looking at me and smiling, and other people at their windows, and I'm so angry I bawl at them too. I say, 'I have absolute and perfect right to be in the street same as anybody else, and I have absolute and perfect right to ask the police why they don't even look for my money when it disappear. 13

It's because a dam' English thief take it you don't look,' I say. The end of all this is that I have to go before a magistrate, and he fine me five pounds for drunk and disorderly, and he give me two weeks to pay.

When I get back from the court I walk up and down the kitchen, up and down, waiting for six o'clock because I have no five pounds left, and I don't know what to do. I telephone at six and a woman answers me very short and sharp, then Mr Sims comes along and he don't sound too pleased either when I tell him what happen. 'Oh Lord!' he says, and I say I'm sorry. 'Well, don't panic,' he says, 'I'll pay the fine. But look, I don't think . . .' Then he breaks off and talk to some other person in the room. He goes on, 'Perhaps better not stay at No. 17. I think I can arrange something else. I'll call for you Wednesday – Saturday latest. Now behave till then.' And he hang up before I can answer that I don't want to wait till Wednesday, much less Saturday. I want to get out of that house double quick and with no delay. First I think I ring back, then I think better not as he sound so vex.

I get ready, but Wednesday he don't come, and Saturday he don't come. All the week I stay in the flat. Only once I go out and arrange for bread, milk and eggs to be left at the door, and seems to me I meet up with a lot of policemen. They don't look at me, but they see me all right I don't want to drink – I'm all the time listening, listening and thinking, how can I leave before I know if my fine is paid? I tell myself the police let me know, that's certain. But I don't trust them. What they care? The answer is Nothing. Nobody care. One afternoon I knock at the old lady's flat upstairs, because I get the idea she give me good advice. I can hear her moving about and talking, but she don't answer and I never try again.

Nearly two weeks pass like that, then I telephone. It's the woman speaking and she say, 'Mr Sims is not in London at present.' I ask, 'When will he be back – it's urgent,' and she hang up. I'm not surprised. Not at all. I knew that would happen. All the same I feel heavy like lead. Near the phone box is a chemist's shop, so I ask him for something to make me sleep, the day is bad enough, but to lie awake all night – Ah no! He gives me a little bottle marked 'One or two tablets only' and I take three when I go to bed because more and more I think that sleeping is better than no matter what else. However, I lie there, eyes wide open as usual, so I take three more. Next thing I know the room is full of sunlight, so it must be late afternoon, but the lamp is still on. My head turn around and I can't think well at all. At first I ask myself how I get to the place. Then it comes to me, but in pictures – like the landlady kicking my dress, and when I take my ticket at Victoria Station, and Mr Sims telling me to eat the sandwiches, but I can't remember everything clear, and I feel very giddy and sick. I take in the milk and eggs at the door, go in the kitchen, and try to eat but the food hard to swallow.

It's when I'm putting the things away that I see the bottles – pushed back on the lowest shelf in the cupboard.

There's a lot of drink left, and I'm glad I tell you. Because I can't bear the way I feel. Not any more. I mix a gin and vermouth and I drink it quick, then I mix another and drink it slow by the window. The garden looks different, like I never see it before. I know quite well what I must do, but it's late now – tomorrow I have one more drink, of wine this time, and then a song comes in my head, I sing it and I dance it, and more I sing, more I am sure this is the

best tune that has ever come to me in all my life.

The sunset light from the window is gold colour. My shoes sound loud on the boards. So I take them off, my stockings too, and go on dancing but the room feel shut in, I can't breathe, and I go outside still singing. Maybe I dance a bit too. I forget all about that woman till I hear her saying, 'Henry, look at this.' I turn around and I see her at the window. 'Oh yes, I wanted to speak with you,' I say. 'Why bring the police and get me in bad trouble? Tell me that.'

'And you tell me what you're doing here at all,' she says. 'This is a respectable neighbourhood.'

Then the man come along. 'Now, young woman, take yourself off. You ought to be ashamed of this behaviour.'

'It's disgraceful,' he says, talking to his wife, but loud so I can hear, and she speaks loud too – for once. 'At least the other tarts that crook installed here were *white* girls,' she says.

'You a dam' fouti liar,' I say. 'Plenty of those girls in your country already. Numberless as the sands on the shore. You don't need me for that.'

'You're not a howling success at it certainly.' Her voice sweet sugar again. 'And you won't be seeing much more of your friend Mr Sims. He's in trouble too. Try somewhere else. Find somebody else. If you can, of course.' When she say that my arm moves of itself. I pick up a stone and bam! through the window. Not the one they are standing at but the next, which is of coloured glass, green and purple and yellow.

I never see a woman look so surprise. Her mouth fall open she so full of surprise. I start to laugh, louder and louder – I laugh like my grandmother, with my hands on my hips and my head back. (When she laugh like that you can hear her to the end of our street.) At last I say, 'Well, I'm sorry. An accident. I get it fixed tomorrow early.' 'That glass is irreplaceable,' the man says. 'Irreplaceable.' 'Good thing,' I say, 'those colours look like they sea-sick to me. I buy you a better windowglass.'

He shake his fist at me. 'You won't be let off with a fine this time,' he says. Then they draw the curtains, I call out at them. 'You run away. Always you run away. Ever since I come here you hunt me down because I don't answer back. It's you shameless.' I try to sing 'Don't trouble me now'.

Don't trouble me now
You without honour.

> Don't walk in my footstep
> You without shame.

But my voice don't sound right, so I get back indoors and drink one more glass of wine – still wanting to laugh, and still thinking of my grandmother for that is one of her songs.

It's about a man whose doudou give him the go-by when she find somebody rich and he sail away to Panama. Plenty people die there of fever when they make that Panama canal so long ago. But he don't die. He come back with dollars and the girl meet him on the jetty, all dressed up and smiling. Then he sing to her, 'You without honour, you without shame'. It sound good in Martinique patois too: 'Sans honte'.

Afterwards I ask myself, 'Why I do that? It's not like me. But if they treat you wrong over and over again the hour strike when you burst out that's what.'

Too besides, Mr Sims can't tell me now I have no spirit. I don't care, I sleep quickly and I'm glad I break the woman's ugly window. But as to my own song it go *right* away and it never come back. A pity.

Next morning the doorbell ringing wake me up.

The people upstairs don't come down, and the bell keeps on like fury self. So I go to look, and there is a policeman and a policewoman outside. As soon as I open the door the woman put her foot in it. She wear sandals and thick stockings and I never see a foot so big or so bad. It look like it want to mash up the whole world. Then she come in after the foot, and her face not so pretty either. The policeman tell me my fine is not paid and people make serious complaints about me, so they're taking me back to the magistrate. He show me a paper and I look at it, but I don't read it. The woman push me in the bedroom, and tell me to get dress quickly, but I just stare at her, because I think perhaps I wake up soon. Then I ask her what I must wear. She say she suppose I had some clothes on yesterday. Or not? 'What's it matter, wear anything,' she says. But I find clean underclothes and stockings and my shoes with high heels and I comb my hair. I start to file my nails, because I think they too long for magistrate's court but she get angry. 'Are you coming quietly or aren't you?' she says. So I go with them and we get in a car outside.

I wait for a long time in a room full of policemen. They come in, they go out, they telephone, they talk in low voices. Then it's my turn, and first thing I notice in the court room is a man with frowning black eyebrows. He sit below the magistrate, he dressed in black and he so handsome I can't take my eyes off him. When he see that he frowns worse than before.

First comes a policeman to testify I cause disturbance, and then comes the old gentleman from next door. He repeat that bit about nothing but the truth so help me God. Then he says I make dreadful noise at night and use abominable language, and dance in obscene fashion. He says when they try to shut the curtains because his wife so terrify of me, I throw stones and break a valuable stain-glass window. He say his wife get serious injury if she'd been hit, and as it is she in terrible nervous condition and the doctor is with her. I think, 'Believe me, if I aim at your wife I hit your wife – that's certain.' 'There was no provocation,' he says. 'None at all.' Then another lady from across the street says this is true. She heard no provocation whatsoever, and she swear that they shut the curtains but I go on insulting them and using filthy language and she saw all this and heard it.

The magistrate is a little gentleman with a quiet

voice, but I'm very suspicious of these quiet voices now. He ask me why I don't pay any fine, and I say because I haven't the money. I get the idea they want to find out all about Mr Sims – they listen so very attentive. But they'll find out nothing from me. He ask how long I have the flat and I say I don't remember. I know they want to trip me up like they trip me up about my savings so I won't answer. At last he ask if I have anything to say as I can't be allowed to go on being a nuisance. I think, 'I'm nuisance to you because I have no money that's all.' I want to speak up and tell him how they steal all my savings, so when my landlord asks for month's rent I haven't got it to give. I want to tell him the woman next door provoke me since long time and call me bad names but she have a soft sugar voice and nobody hear – that's why I broke her window, but I'm ready to buy another after all. I want to say all I do is sing in that old garden, and I want to say this in decent quiet voice. But I hear myself talking loud and I see my hands wave in the air. Too besides it's no use, they won't believe me, so I don't finish. I stop, and I feel the tears on my face. 'Prove it.' That's all they will say. They whisper, they whisper. They nod, they nod.

Next thing I'm in a car again with a different policewoman, dressed very smart. Not in uniform. I ask her where she's taking me and she says 'Holloway' just that 'Holloway'.

I catch hold of her hand because I'm afraid. But she takes it away. Cold and smooth her hand slide away and her face is china face – smooth like a doll and I think, 'This is the last time I ask anything from anybody. So help me God.'

The car come up to a black castle and little mean streets are all round it. A lorry was blocking up the castle gates. When it get by we pass through and I am in jail. First I stand in a line with others who are waiting to give up handbags and all belongings to a woman behind bars like in a post office. The girl in front bring out a nice compact, look like gold to me, lipstick to match and a wallet full of notes. The woman keep the money, but she give back the powder and lipstick and she half-smile. I have two pounds seven shillings and sixpence in pennies. She take my purse, then she throw me my compact (which is cheap) my comb and my handkerchief like everything in my bag is dirty. So I think, 'Here too, here too.' But I tell myself, 'Girl, what you expect, eh? They all like that. All.'

Some of what happen afterwards I forget, or perhaps better not remember. Seems to me they start by trying to frighten you. But they don't succeed with me for I don't care for nothing now, it's as if my heart hard like a rock and I can't feel.

Then I'm standing at the top of a staircase with a lot of women and girls. As we are going down I notice the railing very low on one side, very easy to jump, and a long way below there's the grey stone passage like it's waiting for you.

As I'm thinking this a uniform woman step up alongside quick and grab my arm. She say, 'Oh no you don't.'

I was just noticing the railing very low that's all – but what's the use of saying so.

Another long line waits for the doctor. It move forward slowly and my legs terrible tired. The girl in front is very young and she cry and cry. 'I'm scared,' she keeps saying. She's lucky in a way – as for me I never will cry again. It all dry up and hard in me now. That, and a lot besides. In the end I tell her to stop, because she doing just what these people want her to do.

She stop crying and start a long story, but while she is speaking her voice get very far away, and I find I can't see her face clear at all.

Then I'm in a chair, and one of those uniform women is pushing my head down between my knees, but let her push – everything go away from me just the same.

They put me in the hospital because the doctor say I'm sick. I have cell by myself and it's all right except I don't sleep. The things they say you mind I don't mind.

When they clang the door on me I think, 'You shut me in, but you shut all those other dam' devils *out*. They can't reach me now.'

At first it bothers me when they keep on looking at me all through the night. They open a little window in the doorway to do this. But I get used to it and get used to the night chemise they give me. It very thick, and to my mind it not very clean either – but what's that matter to me? Only the food I can't swallow – especially the porridge. The woman ask me sarcastic, 'Hunger striking?' But afterwards I can leave most of it, and she don't say nothing.

One day a nice girl comes around with books and she give me two, but I don't want to read so much. Beside one is about a murder, and the other is about a ghost and I don't think it's at all like those books tell you.

There is nothing I want now. It's no use. If they leave me in peace and quiet that's all I ask. The window is barred but not small, so I can see a little thin tree through the bars, and I like watching it.

After a week they tell me I'm better and I can go out with the others for exercise. We walk round and round one of the yards in that castle – it is fine weather and the sky is a kind of pale blue, but the yard is a terrible sad place. The sunlight fall down and die there. I get tired walking in high heels and I'm glad when that's over.

We can talk, and one day an old woman come up and ask me for dog-ends. I don't understand, and she start muttering at me like she very vexed. Another woman tell me she mean cigarette ends, so I say I don't smoke. But the old woman still look angry, and when we're going in she give me one push and I nearly fall down. I'm glad to get away from these people, and hear the door clang and take my shoes off.

Sometimes I think, 'I'm here because I wanted to sing,' and I have to laugh. But there's a small looking glass in my cell and I see myself and I'm like somebody else. Like some strange new person. Mr

Sims tell me I too thin, but what he say now to this person in the looking glass? So I don't laugh again.

Usually I don't think at all. Everything and everybody seem small and far away, that is the only trouble.

Twice the doctor come to see me. He don't say much and I don't say anything, because a uniform woman is always there. She looks like she thinking, 'Now the lies start.' So I prefer not to speak. Then I'm sure they can't trip me up. Perhaps I there still, or in a worse place. But one day this happen.

We were walking round and round in the yard and I hear a woman singing – the voice come from high up, from one of the small barred windows. At first I don't believe it. Why should anybody sing here? Nobody want to sing in jail, nobody want to do anything. There's no reason, and you have no hope. I think I must be asleep, dreaming, but I'm awake all right and I see all the others are listening too. A nurse is with us that afternoon, not a policewoman. She stop and look up at the window.

It's a smoky kind of voice, and a bit rough sometimes as if those old dark walls theyselves are complaining, because they see too much misery – too much. But it don't fall down and die in the courtyard; 27

seems to me it could jump the gates of the jail easy and travel far, and nobody could stop it. I don't hear the words – only the music. She sing one verse and she begin another, then she break off sudden. Everybody starts walking again, and nobody says one word. But as we go in I ask the woman in front who was singing. 'That's the Holloway song,' she says. 'Don't you know it yet? She was singing from the punishment cells, and she tell the girls cheerio and never say die.' Then I have to go one way to the hospital block and she goes another so we don't speak again.

When I'm back in my cell I can't just wait for bed. I walk up and down and I think. 'One day I hear that song on trumpets and these walls will fall and rest.' I want to get out so bad I could hammer on the door, for I know now that anything can happen, and I don't want to stay lock up here and miss it.

Then I'm hungry. I eat everything they bring and in the morning I'm still so hungry I eat the porridge. Next time the doctor come he tells me I seem much better. Then I say a little of what really happen in that house. Not much. Very careful.

He look at me hard and kind of surprised. At the

door he shake his finger and says, 'Now don't let me see you here again.'

That evening the woman tells me I'm going, but she's so upset about it I don't ask questions. Very early, before it's light she bangs the door open and shouts at me to hurry up. As we're going along the passages I see the girl who gave me the books. She's in a row with others doing exercises. Up Down, Up Down, Up. We pass quite close and I notice she's looking very pale and tired. It's crazy, it's all crazy. This up down business and everything else too. When they give me my money I remember I leave my compact in the cell, so I ask if I can go back for it. You should see that policewoman's face as she shoo me on.

There's no car, there's a van and you can't see through the windows. The third time it stop I get out with one other, a young girl, and it's the same magistrates' court as before.

The two of us wait in a small room, nobody else there, and after a while the girl say, 'What the hell are they doing? I don't want to spend all day here.' She go to the bell and she keep her finger press on it. When I look at her she say, 'Well, what are they *for*?' That girl's face is hard like a board – she could change faces with many and you wouldn't know the difference. But she get results certainly. A policeman comes in, all smiling, and we go in the court. The same magistrate, the same frowning man sits below, and when I hear my fine is paid I want to ask who paid it, but he yells at me, 'Silence.'

I think I will never understand the half of what happen, but they tell me I can go, and I understand that. The magistrate ask if I'm leaving the neighbourhood and I say yes, then I'm out in the streets again, and it's the same fine weather, same feeling I'm dreaming.

When I get to the house I see two men talking in the garden. The front door and the door of the flat are both open. I go in, and the bedroom is empty, nothing but the glare streaming inside because they take the Venetian blinds away. As I'm wondering where my suitcase is, and the clothes I leave in the wardrobe, there's a knock and it's the old lady from upstairs carrying my case packed, and my coat is over her arm. She says she sees me come in. 'I kept your things for you.' I start to thank her but she turn her back and walk away. They like that here, and better not expect too much. Too besides, I bet they tell her I'm terrible person.

I go in the kitchen, but when I see they are cutting down the big tree at the back I don't stay to watch.

At the station I'm waiting for the train and a woman asks if I feel well. 'You look so tired,' she says. 'Have you come a long way?' I want to answer, 'I come so far I lose myself on that journey.' But I tell her, 'Yes, I am quite well. But I can't stand the heat.' She says she can't stand it either, and we talk about the weather till the train come in.

I'm not frightened of them any more – after all what else can they do? I know what to say and everything go like a clock works.

I get a room near Victoria where the landlady accept one pound in advance, and next day I find a job in the kitchen of a private hotel close by. But I don't stay there long. I hear of another job going in a big store – altering ladies' dresses and I get that. I lie and tell them I work in very expensive New York shop. I speak bold and smooth faced, and they never check up on me. I make a friend there – Clarice – very light coloured, very smart, she have a lot to do with the customers and she laugh at some of them behind their backs. But I say it's not their fault if the dress don't fit. Special dress for one person only –

that's very expensive in London. So it's take in, or let out, all the time. Clarice have two rooms not far from the store. She furnish herself gradual and she gives parties sometimes Saturday nights. It's there I start whistling the Holloway Song. A man comes up to me and says, 'Let's hear that again.' So I whistle it again (I never sing now) and he tells me 'Not bad'. Clarice have an old piano somebody give her to store and he plays the tune, jazzing it up. I say, 'No, not like that,' but everybody else say the way he do it is first class. Well I think no more of this till I get a letter from him telling me he has sold the song and as I was quite a help he encloses five pounds with thanks.

I read the letter and I could cry. For after all, that song was all I had. I don't belong nowhere really, and I haven't money to buy my way to belonging. I don't want to either.

But when that girl sing, she sing to me and she sing for me. I was there because I was *meant* to be there. It was *meant* I should hear it – this I *know*.

Now I've let them play it wrong, and it will go from me like all the other songs – like everything. Nothing left for me at all.

But then I tell myself all this is foolishness. Even

if they played it on trumpets, even if they played it just right, like I wanted — no walls would fall so soon. 'So let them call it jazz,' I think, and let them play it wrong. That won't make no difference to the song I heard.

I buy myself a dusty pink dress with the money.

Outside the Machine

The big clinic near Versailles was run on strictly English lines, so every morning the patients in the women's general ward were woken up at six. They had tea and bread-and-butter. Then they lay and waited while the nurses brought tin basins and soap. When they had washed they lay and waited again.

There were fifteen beds in the tall, narrow room. The walls were painted grey. The windows were long but high up, so that you could see only the topmost branches of the trees in the grounds outside. Through the glass the sky had no colour.

At half-past ten the matron, attended by a sister, came in to inspect the ward, walking as though she were royalty opening a public building. She stopped every now and again, glanced at a patient's temperature chart here, said a few words there. The young woman in the last bed but one on the left-hand side was a newcomer. 'Best, Inez,' the chart said.

'You came last evening, didn't you?'

'Yes.'

'Quite comfortable?'

'Oh yes, quite.'

'Can't you do without all those things while you are here?' the matron asked, meaning the rouge, powder, lipstick and hand-mirror on the bed table.

'It's so that I shouldn't look too awful, because then I always feel much worse.'

But the matron shook her head and walked on without smiling, and Inez drew the sheets up to her chin, feeling bewildered and weak. *I'm cold, I'm tired.*

'Has anyone ever told you that you're very much like Raquel Meller?' the old lady in the next bed said. She was sitting up, wrapped in a black shawl embroidered with pink and yellow flowers.

'Am I? Oh, am I really?'

'Yes, very much like.'

'Do you think so?' Inez said.

The tune of *La Violetera*, Raquel Meller's song, started up in her head. She felt happier – then quite happy and rather gay. 'Why should I be so damned sad?' she thought. 'It's ridiculous. The day after I come out of this place something lucky might happen.'

And it was not so bad lying here and having everything done for you. It was only when you moved that you got frightened because you couldn't imagine ever moving again without hurting yourself.

She looked at the row of beds opposite and sighed. 'It's rum here, isn't it?'

'Oh, you'll feel different tomorrow,' the old lady said. She spoke English hesitatingly – not with an accent, but as if her tongue were used to another language.

The two talked a good deal that day, off and on.

'. . . And how was I to know,' Inez complained, 'that, on top of everything else, my inside would go *kaput* like this? And of course it must happen at the wrong time.'

'Now, shut up,' she told herself, 'shut up. Don't say, "Just when I haven't any money." Don't give yourself away. What a fool you are!' But she could not stop the flood of words.

At intervals the old lady clicked her tongue compassionately or said 'Poor child'. She had a broad, placid face. Her hair was black – surely dyed, Inez thought. She wore two rings with coloured stones on the third finger of her left hand and one – a thick
gold ring carved into an indistinguishable pattern –

on the little finger. There was something wrong with her knee, it appeared, and she had tried several other hospitals.

'French hospitals are more easy-going, but I was very lucky to get into this place, it has quite a reputation. There's nothing like English nursing. And, considering what you get, you pay hardly anything. An English matron, a resident English doctor, several of the nurses are English. I believe the private rooms are *most* luxurious, but of course they are very expensive.'

Her name was Tavernier. She had left England as a young girl and had never been back. She had been married twice. Her first husband was a bad man, her second husband was a good man. Just like that. Her second husband was a good man who had left her a little money.

When she talked about the first husband you could tell that she still hated him, after all those years. When she talked about the good one tears came into her eyes. She said that they were perfectly happy, completely happy, never an unkind word and tears came into her eyes.

'Poor old mutt,' Inez thought, 'she really has persuaded herself to believe that.'

Madame Tavernier said in a low voice, 'Do you know what he said in the last letter he wrote to me? "You are everything to me." Yes, that's what he said in the last letter I had.'

'Poor old mutt,' Inez thought again.

Madame Tavernier wiped her eyes. Her face looked calm and gentle, as if she were repeating to herself, 'Nobody can say this isn't true, because I've got the letter and I can show it.'

The fat, fair woman in the bed opposite was also chatting with her neighbour. They were both blonde, very clean and aggressively respectable. For some reason they fitted in so well with their surroundings that they made everyone else seem dubious, out of place. The fat one discussed the weather, and her neighbour's answers were like an echo. 'Hot . . . oh yes, very hot . . . hotter than yesterday . . . yes, much hotter . . . I wish the weather would break . . . yes, I wish it would, but no chance of that . . . no, I suppose not . . . oh, rather fancy so . . .'

Under cover of this meaningless conversation the fair woman's stare at Inez was sharp, sly and inquisitive. 'An English person? English, what sort of English? To which of the seven divisions, sixty-nine subdivisions, and thousand-and-three subsubdivisions do you belong? (*But only one sauce, damn you.*) My world is a stable, decent world. If you withhold information, or if you confuse me by jumping from one category to another, I can be extremely disagreeable, and I am not without subtlety and inventive powers when I want to be disagreeable. Don't underrate me. I have set the machine in motion and crushed many like you. Many like you . . .'

Madame Tavernier shifted uneasily in her bed, as if she sensed this clash of personalities – stares meeting in mid-air, sparks flying . . .

'Those two ladies just opposite are English,' she whispered.

'Oh, are they?'

'And so is the one in the bed on the other side of you.'

'The sleepy one they make such a fuss about?'

'She's a dancer – a "girl", you know. One of the Yetta Kauffman girls. She's had an operation for appendicitis.'

'Oh, has she?'

'The one with the screen round her bed,' Madame Tavernier chattered on, 'is very ill. She's not expected to – And the one . . .'

Inez interrupted after a while. 'They seem to have stuck all the English down this end, don't they? I wish they had mixed us up a bit more.'

'They never do,' Madame Tavernier answered. 'I've often noticed it.'

'It's a mistake,' said Inez. 'English people are usually pleasanter to foreigners than they are to each other.'

After a silence Madame Tavernier inquired politely, 'Have you travelled a lot?'

'Oh, a bit.'

'And do you like it here?'

'Yes, I like Paris much the best.'

'I suppose you feel at home,' Madame Tavernier said. Her voice was ironical. 'Like many people. There's something for every taste.'

'No, I don't feel particularly at home. That's not why I like it.'

She turned away and shut her eyes. She knew the pain was going to start again. And, sure enough, it did. They gave her an injection and she went to sleep.

Next morning she woke feeling dazed. She lay and watched two nurses charging about, very brisk and busy and silent. They did not even say 'Come along', or 'Now, now', or 'Drink that up'.

They moved about surely and quickly. They did everything in an impersonal way. They were like parts of a machine, she thought, that was working smoothly. The women in the beds bobbed up and down and in and out. They too were parts of a machine. They had a strength, a certainty, because all their lives they had belonged to the machine and worked smoothly, in and out, just as they were told. Even if the machine got out of control, even if it went mad, they would still work in and out, just as they were told, whirling smoothly, faster and faster, to destruction.

She lay very still, so that nobody should know she was afraid. Because she was outside the machine they might come along any time with a pair of huge iron tongs and pick her up and put her on the rubbish heap, and there she would lie and rot. 'Useless, this one,' they would say; and throw her away before she could explain, 'It isn't like you think it is, not at all. It isn't like they say it is. Wait a bit and let me explain. You must listen; it's very important.'

But in the evening she felt better.

The girl in the bed on the right, who was sitting up, said she wanted to write to a friend at the theatre.

'In French,' she said. 'Can anybody write the letter for me, because I don't know French?'

'I'll write it for you,' Madame Tavernier offered.

'"Dear Lili . . . L-i-l-i. Dear Lili . . ." well, say, "I'm getting on all right again. Come and see me on Monday or Thursday. Any time from two to four. And when you come will you bring me some note-paper and stamps? I hope it won't be long before I get out of this place. I'll tell you about that on Monday. Don't forget the stamps. Tell the others that they can come to see me, and tell them how to get here. Your affectionate friend, and so on, Pat." Give it to me and I'll sign it . . . Thanks.'

The girl's voice had two sounds in it. One was clear and light, the other heavy and ruthless.

'You seem to be having a rotten time, you in the next bed,' she said.

'I feel better now.'

'Have you been in Paris long?'

'I live here.'

'Ah, then you'll be having your pals along to cheer you up.'

'I don't think so. I don't expect anybody.'

The girl stared. She was not much over twenty and her clear blue eyes slanted upwards a little. She looked as if, standing up, she would be short with sturdy dancer's legs. Stocky, like a little pony.

Oh God, let her go on talking about herself and not looking at me, or sizing me up, or anything like that.

'This French girl, this friend of mine, she's a perfect scream,' Pat said. 'But she's an awfully obliging girl. If I say, 'Turn up with stamps,' she will turn up with stamps. That's why I'm writing to her and not to one of our lot. Our lot might turn up or they might not. You know. But she's a perfect scream, really . . . As a matter of fact, she's not bad-looking, but the way she walks is too funny. She's a *femme nue*, and they've taught her to walk like that. It's all right without shoes, but with shoes it's – well . . . you'll see when she comes here. They only get paid half what we do, too. Anyway, she's an awfully obliging kid; she's a sweet kid, poor devil.'

A nurse brought in supper.

'The girls are nice and the actors are nice,' Pat went on, 'but the stage hands hate us. Isn't it funny? You see, one of them tried to kiss one of our lot and she smacked his face. He looked sort of surprised, 43 she said. And then do you know what he did? He hit her back! Well, and do you know what we did? We said to the stage manager, "If that man doesn't get the sack, we won't go on." They tried one show without us and then they gave in. The principals whose numbers were spoilt made a hell of a row. The French girls can't do our stuff because they can't keep together. They're all right alone – very good sometimes, but they don't understand team work. . . . And now, my God, the stage hands don't half hate us. We have to go in twos to the lavatory. And yet, the girls and the actors are awfully nice; it's only the stage hands who hate us.'

The fat woman opposite – her name was Mrs Wilson – listened to all this, at first suspiciously, then approvingly. Yes, this is permissible; it has its uses. Pretty English chorus girl – north country – with a happy, independent disposition and bright, teasing eyes. Placed! All correct.

Pat finished eating and then went off to sleep again very suddenly, like a child.

'A saucy girl, isn't she?' Madame Tavernier said. Her eyes were half-shut, the corners of her mouth turned downwards.

Through the windows the light turned from dim

yellow to mauve, from mauve to grey, from grey to black. Then it was dark except for the unshaded bulbs tinted red all along the ward. Inez put her arm round her head and turned her face to the pillow.

'Good night,' the old lady said. And after a long while she said, 'Don't cry, don't cry.'

Inez whispered, 'They kill you so slowly . . .'

The ward was a long, grey river; the beds were ships in a mist . . .

The next day was Sunday. Even through those window panes the sky looked blue, and the sun made patterns on the highly polished floor. The patients had breakfast half an hour later – seven instead of half-past six.

'Only milk for you today,' the nurse said. Inez was going to ask why; then she remembered that her operation was fixed for Monday. *Don't think of it yet. There's still quite a long time to go.*

After the midday meal the matron told them that an English clergyman was going to visit the ward and hold a short service if nobody minded. Nobody did mind, and after a while the parson came in through an unsuspected door, looking as if he felt very cold, as if he had never been warm in his life. He had grey hair and a shy, shut-in face.

He stood at the end of the ward and the patients turned their heads to look at him. The screen round the bed on the other side had been taken away and the yellow-faced, shrunken woman who lay there turned her head like the others and looked.

The clergyman said a prayer and most of the patients said 'Amen'. ('Amen,' they said. 'We are listening,' they said ... I am poor bewildered unhappy comfort me I am dying console me of course I don't let on that I know I'm dying but I know I know Don't talk about life as it is because it has nothing to do with me now Say something go on say something because I'm so darned sick of women's voices Christ how I hate women Say something funny that I can laugh at but anything you say will be funny you old geezer you Never mind say something ... 'We are listening,' they said, 'we are listening. ...') But the parson was determined to stick to life as it is, for his address was a warning against those vices which would antagonize their fellows and make things worse for them. Self-pity, for instance. Where does that lead you? Ah, where? Cynicism. So cheap ... Rebellion. So useless ... 'Let us remember,' he ended, 'that God is a just God and that man, made in His image, is also just. On the whole. And

so, dear sisters, let us try to live useful, righteous and
God-fearing lives in that state to which it has pleased
Him to call us. Amen.'

He said another prayer and then went round shaking hands. 'How do you do, how do you do, how do
you do?' All along the two lines. Then he went out
again.

After he had gone there was silence in the ward
for a few seconds, then somebody sighed.

Madame Tavernier remarked, 'Poor little man, he
was so nervous.'

'Well, it didn't last long, anyway,' Pat said. 'On
and off like the Demon King . . .'

> 'Oh, he doesn't look much like a lover,
> But you can't tell a book by its cover.'

Then she sang *The Sheik of Araby*. She tied a
towel round her head for a turban and began again:
'Over the desert wild and free . . . Sing up, girls,
chorus. I'm the Sheik of Arabee . . .'

Everybody looked at Pat and laughed; the dying
woman's small yellow face was convulsed with
laughter.

'There's lots of time before tomorrow,' Inez
thought. 'I needn't bother about it yet.'

'I'm the Sheik of Arabee ...' Somebody was singing it in French – '*Je cherche Antinéa.*' It was a curious translation – significant when you came to think of it.

Pat shouted, 'Listen to this. Anybody recognize it? Old but good. "Who's that knocking at my door? said the fair young ladye . . ."'

The tall English sister came in. She had a narrow face, small deep-set eyes of an unusual reddish-brown colour and a large mouth. Her pale lips lay calmly one on the other, as if she were very good-tempered, or perhaps very self-controlled. She smiled blandly and said, 'Now then, Pat, you must stop this,' arranged the screen round the bed on the other side and pulled down the blind of the window at the back.

It was really very hot and after she had gone out again most of the women lay in a coma, but Pat went on talking. The sound of her own voice seemed to excite her. She became emphatic, as if someone was arguing with her.

She talked about love and the difference between glamour and dirt. The real difference was £–s–d, she said. If there was some money about there could be some glamour; otherwise, say what you liked, it was simply dirty – as well as foolish.

'Plenty of survival value there,' Inez thought. She lay with her eyes closed, trying to see trees and smooth water. But the pictures she made slipped through her mind too quickly, so that they became distorted and malignant.

That night everybody in the ward was wakeful. Somebody moaned. The nurse rushed about with a bed pan, grumbling under her breath.

2

At nine o'clock on Monday morning the tall English sister was saying, 'You'll be quite all right. I'm going to give you a morphine injection now.'

After this Inez was still frightened, but in a much duller way.

'I hope you'll be there,' she said drowsily. But there was another nurse in the operating room. She was wearing a mask and she looked horrible, Inez thought – like a torturer.

Floating in the air, which was easy and natural after the morphine – *Of course, I've always been able to do this. Why did I ever forget? How stupid of me!* – she watched herself walking across the floor with tears streaming down her cheeks, supported by the terrifying stranger.

'Now, don't be silly,' the nurse said irritably.

Inez sat down on the edge of the couch, not floating now, not divided. One, and heavy as lead.

'You don't know why I'm crying,' she thought.

She tried to look at the sky, but there was a mist before her eyes and she could not see it. She felt hands pressing hard on her shoulders.

'No, no, no, leave her alone,' somebody said in French.

The English doctor was not there – only this man, who was also wearing a mask.

'They're so stupid,' Inez said in a high, complaining voice. 'It's terrible. Oh, what's going to happen, what's going to happen?'

'Don't be afraid,' the doctor said. His brown eyes looked kind. 'N'ayez pas peur, n'ayez pas peur.'

'All right,' Inez said, and lay down.

The English doctor's voice said, 'Now breathe deeply. Count slowly. One – two – three – four – five – six . . .'

3

'Do you feel better today?' the old lady asked.

'Yes, much better.'

The blind at the back of her bed was down. It tapped a bit. She was sleepy; she felt as if she could sleep for weeks.

'Hullo,' said Pat, 'come to life again?'

'I'm much better now.'

'You've been awfully bad,' Pat said. 'You were awfully ill on Monday, weren't you?'

'Yes, I suppose I was.'

The screen which had been up round her bed for three days had shut her away even from her hand mirror; and now she took it up and looked at herself as if she were looking at a stranger. She had lain seeing nothing but a succession of pictures of the past, always sinister, always too highly coloured, always distorted. She had heard nothing but the incoherent, interminable conversation in her head.

'I look different,' she thought.

'I look awful,' she thought, staring anxiously at her thin, grey face and the hollows under her eyes. 51

This was very important; her principal asset was threatened.

'I must rest,' she thought. 'Rest, not worry.'

She passed her powder puff over her face and put some rouge on.

Pat was watching her. 'D'you know what I've noticed? People who look ghastly oughtn't to put makeup on. You only look worse if you aren't all right underneath – much older. My pal Lili came along on Monday. You should have seen how pretty she looked. I will say for these Paris girls they do know how to make up . . .'

Yap, yap, yap . . .

'Even if they aren't anything much – and often they aren't, mind you – they know how to make themselves look all right. I mean, you see prettier girls in London, but in my opinion . . .'

The screen round the bed on the opposite side had been taken away. The bed was empty. Inez looked at it and said nothing. Madame Tavernier, who saw her looking at it, also said nothing, but for a moment her eyes were frightened.

4

The next day the ward sister brought in some English novels.

'You'll find these very soothing,' she said, and there was a twinkle in her eye. A splendid nurse, that one; she knew her job. What they call a born nurse.

A born nurse, as they say. Or you could be a born cook, or a born clown or a born fool, a born this, a born that . . .

'What's the joke now?' Pat asked suspiciously.

'Oh, nothing. I was thinking how hard it is to believe in free will.'

'I suppose you know what you're talking about,' Pat answered coldly. She had become hostile for some reason. Not that it mattered.

'Everything will be all right; I needn't worry,' Inez assured herself. 'There's still heaps of time.'

And soon she believed it. Lying there, being looked after and waking obediently at dawn, she began to feel like a child, as if the future would surely be pleasant, though it was hardly conceivable. It was as if she had always lain there and had known everyone else in the ward all her life – Madame Tavernier, her shawl, her rings, her crochet and her travel books, Pat and her repertoire of songs, the two fair, fat women who always looked so sanctimonious when they washed.

The room was wide and the beds widely spaced, but now she knew something of the others too. There was a mysterious girl with long plaits and a sullen face who sometimes helped the nurse to make the beds in the morning – mysterious because there did not seem to be anything the matter with her. She ought to have been pretty, but she always kept her head down and if by chance you met her eyes she would blink and glance away. And there was the one who wore luxury pyjamas, the one who knitted, the other constant reader – watching her was sometimes a frightening game – the one who had a great many visitors, the ugly one, rather like a monkey, who all day sewed something that looked like a pink crêpe-de-chine chemise.

But her dreams were uneasy, and if a book fell or a door banged her heart would jump – a painful echo. And she found herself disliking some of the novels the sister brought. One day when she was reading her face reddened with anger. *Why, it's not a bit like that. My Lord, what liars these people are!*

And nobody to stand up and tell them so. Yah, Judas! Thinks it's the truth! You're telling me.

She glanced sideways. Pat, who was staring at her, laughed, raised her eyebrows and tapped her forehead. Inez laughed back, also tapped her forehead and a moment afterwards was reading again, peacefully.

The days were like that, but when night came she burrowed into the middle of the earth to sleep. 'Never wake up, never wake up,' her wise heart told her. But the morning always came, the tin basins, the smell of soap, the long, sunlit, monotonous day.

At · last she was well enough to walk into the bathroom by herself. Going there was all right, but coming back her legs gave way and she had to put her hand on the wall of the passage for support. There was a weight round the middle of her body which was dragging her to earth.

She got back into bed again. Darkness, quiet, safety – all the same, it was time to face up to things, to arrange them neatly. 'One, I feel much worse than I expected: two, I must ask the matron tomorrow if I can stay for another week; they won't want me to pay in advance; three, as soon as I know that I'm all right for another week, I must start writing round and trying to raise some money. Fifty francs when I get out! What's fifty francs when you feel like this?'

That night she lay awake for a long time, making plans. But next morning, when the matron came round, she became nervous of a refusal. 'I'll ask her tomorrow for certain.' However, the whole of the next day passed and she did not say a word.

She ate and slept and read soothing English novels about the respectable and the respected and she did not say a word nor write a letter. Any excuse was good enough: 'She doesn't look in a good temper today . . . Oh, the doctor's with her; I don't think he liked me much. (Well, I don't like you much either, old cock; your eyes are too close together.) Today's Friday, not my lucky day . . . I'll write when my head is clearer . . .'

A long brown passage smelling of turpentine led from the ward to the washroom. There were rows of basins along either whitewashed wall, three water closets and two bathrooms at the far end.

Inez went to one of the washbasins. She was carrying a sponge bag. She took out of it soap, a toothbrush, toothpaste and peroxide.

Somebody opened the door stealthily, hesitated

for a moment, then walked past and stood over one of the basins at the far end. It was the sullen girl, the one with the long plaits. She was wearing a blue kimono.

'She does look fed up,' Inez thought.

The girl leant over the basin with both hands on its edge. Was she going to be sick? Then she gave a long, shivering sigh and opened her sponge bag.

Inez turned away without speaking and began to clean her teeth.

The door opened again and a nurse came in and glanced round the washroom. It was curious to see the expression on her plump, pink face change in a few moments from indifference to inquisitiveness, to astonishment, to shocked anger.

Then she ran across the room, shouting, 'Stop that. Come along, Mrs Murphy. Give it up.'

Inez watched them struggling. Something metallic fell to the floor. Mrs Murphy was twisting like a snake.

'Come on, help me, can't you? Hold her arms,' the nurse said breathlessly.

'Oh, leave me alone, leave me alone,' Mrs Murphy wailed. 'Do for God's sake leave me alone. What do you know about it anyway?'

'Go and call the sister. She's in the ward.'

'She's speaking to me,' Inez thought.

'Oh, leave me alone, leave me alone. Oh, please, please, please, please, please, please,' Mrs Murphy sobbed.

'What's she done?' Inez said. 'Why don't you leave her alone?'

As she spoke two other nurses rushed in at the door and flung themselves on Mrs Murphy, who began to scream loudly, with her mouth open and her head back.

Inez held on to the basins, one by one, and got to the door. Then she held on to the door post, then to the wall of the passage. She reached her bed and lay down shaking.

'What's up? What's the matter?' Pat asked excitedly.

'I don't know.'

'Was it Murphy? You're all right, aren't you? We were wondering if it was Murphy, or . . .'

'"Or you," she means,' Inez thought. '"Or you . . ."'

All that evening Pat and the fair woman, Mrs Wilson, who had been very friendly, talked excitedly. It seemed that they knew all about Mrs Murphy. They knew that she had tried the same thing on before. Suddenly, by magic, they seemed to know all about her. And what a thing to do, to try to kill yourself! If it had been a man, now, you might have been a bit sorry. You might have said, 'Perhaps the poor devil has had a rotten time.' But a woman!

'A married woman with two sweet little kiddies.'

'The fool,' said Pat. 'My God, what would you do with a fool like that?'

Mrs Wilson, who had been in the clinic for some time, explained that there was a medicine cupboard just outside the ward.

'It must have been open,' she said. 'In *which* case, somebody will get into a row. Perhaps Murphy got hold of the key. That's where she might get the morphine tablets.'

But Pat was of the opinion – she said she knew it for a fact, a nurse had told her – that Mrs Murphy had had the hypodermic syringe and the tablets hidden for weeks, ever since she had been in the clinic.

'She's one of these idiotic neurasthenics, neurotics, or whatever you call them. She says she's frightened of life, I ask you. That's why she's here. Under observation. And it only shows you how cunning they are, that she managed to hide the things . . .'

'I'm so awfully sorry for her husband,' said Mrs Wilson. 'And her children. So sorry. The poor kiddies, the poor sweet little kiddies ... Oughtn't a woman like that to be hung?'

Even after the lights had been put out they still talked.

'What's she got to be neurasthenic and neurotic about, anyway?' Pat demanded. 'If she has a perfectly good husband and kiddies, what's she got to be neurasthenic and neurotic about?'

Stone and iron, their voices were. One was stone and one was iron ...

Inez interrupted the duet in a tremulous voice. 'Oh, she's neurasthenic, and they've sent her to a place like this to be cured? That was a swell idea. What a place for a cure for neurasthenia! Who thought that up? The perfectly good, kind husband, I suppose.'

Pat said, 'For God's sake! You get on my nerves. Stop always trying to be different from everybody else.'

'Who's everybody else?'

Nobody answered her.

'What a herd of swine they are!' she thought, but no heat of rage came to warm or comfort her. Sized

her up, Pat had. *Why should you care about a girl like
that? She's as stupid as a foot. But not when it comes to
sizing people up, not when it comes to knowing who is
done for. I'm cold, I'm tired, I'm tired, I'm cold.*

The next morning Mrs Murphy appeared in time to
help make the beds. As usual she walked with her
head down and her eyes down and her shoulders
stooped. She went very slowly along the opposite
side of the ward, and everybody stared at her with
hard, inquisitive eyes.

'What are you muttering about, Inez?' Pat said
sharply.

Mrs Murphy and the nurse reached the end of the
row opposite. Then they began the other row. Slowly
they were coming nearer.

'Shut up, it's nothing to do with you,' Inez told
herself, but her cold hands were clenched under the
sheet.

The nurse said, 'Pat, you're well enough to give a
hand, aren't you? I won't be a moment.'

'Idiot,' Inez thought. 'She oughtn't to have gone
away. But they never know what's happening. But
yes, they know. The machine works smoothly, that's
all.'

In silence Pat and Mrs Murphy started pulling and stretching and patting the sheets and pillows.

'Hullo, Pat,' Mrs Murphy said at last in a low voice.

Pat closed her lips with a righteously disgusted expression. They turned the sheet under at the bottom. They smoothed it down at the top. They began to shake the pillows.

Mrs Murphy's face broke up and she started to cry. 'Oh God,' she said, 'they won't let me get out. They won't.'

Pat said, 'Don't snivel over my pillow. People like you make me sick,' and Mrs Wilson laughed like a horse neighing.

The voice and the laughter were so much alike that they might have belonged to the same person. *Greasy and cold, silly and raw, coarse and thin; everything unutterably horrible.*

'Well, here's bad luck to you,' Inez burst out, 'you pair of bitches. Behaving like that to a sad woman! what do you know about her? . . . You hold your head up and curse them back, Mrs Murphy. It'll do you a lot of good.'

Mrs Murphy rushed out of the room sobbing. 'Who was speaking to you?' Pat said.

Inez heard words coming round and full and satisfying out of her mouth – exactly what she thought about them, exactly what they were, exactly what she hoped would happen to them.

'Disgusting,' said Mrs Wilson. 'I *told* you so,' she added triumphantly. 'I knew it, I knew the sort she was from the first.'

At this moment the door opened and the doctor came in accompanied, not as usual by the matron, but by the tall ward sister.

Once more, for a gesture, Inez shouted, 'This and that to the lot of you!' – 'Not the nurse,' she whispered to the pillow, 'I don't mean her.'

Mrs Wilson announced in a loud, clear voice, 'I think that people who use filthy language oughtn't to be allowed to associate with decent people. I think it's a shame that some women are allowed to associate with ladies at all – a shame. It oughtn't to be allowed.'

The doctor blinked, but the sister's long, narrow face was expressionless. The two were round the beds glancing at the temperature charts here, saying a few words there. Best, Inez . . .

The doctor asked, 'Does this hurt you?'

'No.'

'When I press here does it hurt you?'

'No.'

They were very tall, thin and far away. They turned their heads a little and she could not hear what they said. And when she began, 'I wanted to . . .' she saw that they could not hear her either, and stopped.

5

'You can dress in the washroom after lunch,' the sister said next morning.

'Oh, yes?'

There was nothing to be surprised about. So much time had been paid for and now the time was up and she would have to go. There was nothing to be surprised about.

Inez said, 'Would it be possible to stay two or three days longer? I wanted to make some arrangements. It would be more convenient. I was idiotic not to speak about it before.'

The sister's raised eyebrows were very thin – like two thin new moons.

She said, 'I'm sorry, I'm afraid it's not possible.

Why didn't you ask before? I told the doctor yesterday that I don't think you are very strong yet. But we are expecting four patients this evening and several others tomorrow afternoon. Unfortunately we are going to be very full up and he thinks you are well enough to go. You must rest when you get back home. Move as little as possible.'

'Yes, of course,' Inez said; but she thought, 'No, this time I won't be able to pull it off, this time I'm done.' *We wondered if it was Murphy – or you . . .' Well, it's both of us.*

Then her body relaxed and she lay and did not think of anything, for there is peace in despair in exactly the same way as there is despair in peace. Everything in her body relaxed. She did not make any more plans, she just lay there.

They had their midday dinner – roast beef, potatoes and beans, and then a milk pudding. Just like England. Inez ate and enjoyed it, and then lay back with her arm over her eyes. She knew that Pat was watching her but she lay peaceful, and thought of nothing.

'Here are your things,' the nurse said. 'Will you get dressed now?'

'All right.'

'I'm afraid you're not feeling up to much. Well, you'll have some tea before you go, won't you? And you must go straight to bed as soon as you get back.'

'Get back where?' Inez thought. 'Why should you always take it for granted that everybody has somewhere to get back to?'

'Oh yes,' she said. 'I will.'

And all the time she dressed she saw the street, the 'buses and taxis charging at her, the people jostling her. She heard their voices, saw their eyes ... When you fall you don't ever get up; they take care of that ...

She leant against the wall thinking of Mrs Murphy's voice when she said, 'Please, please, please, please, please ...'

After a while she wiped the tears off her face. She did not put any powder on, and when she got into the ward she could only see the bed she was going to lie on and wait till they came with the tongs to throw her out.

'Will you come over here for a moment?'

There was a chair at the head of each bed. She sat down and looked at the fan-shaped wrinkles under Madame Tavernier's small, dark, melancholy eyes, the swollen blue veins on her hands and the pattern of the gold ring – two roses, the petals touching each other. She read a sentence of the open book lying on the bed: 'De là-haut le paysage qu'on découvre est d'une indiscriptible beauté . . .

Madame Tavernier said, 'That's a charming dress, and you look very nice – very nice indeed.'

'My God!' Inez said. 'That's funny.'

Madame Tavernier whispered, 'S-sh, listen! Turn the chair round. I want to talk to you.'

Inez turned the chair so that her back was towards the rest of the room.

Madame Tavernier took a handkerchief from under her pillow – a white, old-fashioned handkerchief, not small, of very fine linen trimmed with lace. She put it into Inez' hands. 'Here,' she said. 'S-sh . . . here!'

Inez took the handkerchief. It smelled of vanilla. She felt the notes inside it.

'Take care. Don't let the others see. Don't let them notice you crying . . .' She whispered, 'You mustn't mind these people; they don't know anything about life. You mustn't mind them. So many people don't know anything about life . . . so many of them . . . and sometimes I wonder if it isn't getting worse instead of better.' She sighed. 'You hadn't any money, had you?'

Inez shook her head.

'I thought you hadn't. There's enough there for a week or perhaps two. If you are careful.'

'Yes, yes,' Inez said. 'Now I'll be quite all right.'

She stopped crying. She felt tired, rested and rather degraded. She had never taken money from a woman before. She did not like women, she had always told herself, or trust them.

Madame Tavernier went on talking. 'That is quite a lot of money if you use it carefully,' she meant. But that was not what she said.

'Thank you,' Inez said, 'oh, thank you.'

'You'd like some tea before you go, wouldn't you?' the nurse said.

Inez drank the tea, went into the washroom and made up her face. She went back to the old lady's bed.

'Will you give me a kiss?' Madame Tavernier said.

Her powdered skin was soft and flabby as used elastic; it smelt, like her handkerchief, of vanilla. When Inez said, 'I'll never forget your kindness, it's made such a difference to me,' she closed her eyes in a way that meant, 'All right, all right, all right.'

'I'll have a taxi to the station,' Inez decided.

But in the taxi she could only wonder what Madame Tavernier would say if she were suddenly asked what it is like to be old – perhaps she would answer, 'Sometimes it's peaceful' – and remember the gold ring carved into two roses, and above all wish she were back in her bed in the ward with the sheets drawn over her head. Because you can't die and come to life again for a few hundred francs. It takes more than that. It takes more, perhaps, than anybody is ever willing to give.

Audrey began to read. Her book was called *Nothing So Blue*. It was set in the tropics. She started at the paragraph which described the habits of an insect called the jigger.

Almost any book was better than life, Audrey thought. Or rather, life as she was living it. Of course, life would soon change, open out, become quite different. You couldn't go on if you didn't hope that, could you? But for the time being there was no doubt that it was pleasant to get away from it. And books could take her away.

She could give herself up to the written word as naturally as a good dancer to music or a fine swimmer to water. The only difficulty was that after finishing the last sentence she was left with a feeling at once hollow and uncomfortably full. Exactly like indigestion. It was perhaps for this reason that she never forgot that books were one thing and that life was another.

When it came to life Audrey was practical. She

accepted all she was told to accept. And there had been quite a lot of it. She had been in London for the last five years but for one short holiday. There had been the big blitz, then the uneasy lull, then the little blitz, now the fly bombs. But she still accepted all she was told to accept, tried to remember all she was told to remember. The trouble was that she could not always forget all she was told to forget. She could not forget, for instance, that on her next birthday she would be twenty-nine years of age. Not a Girl any longer. Not really. The war had already gobbled up several years and who knew how long it would go on. Audrey dreaded growing old. She disliked and avoided old people and thought with horror of herself as old. She had never told anyone her real and especial reason for loathing the war. She had never spoken of it – even to her friend Monica.

Monica, who was an optimist five years younger than Audrey, was sure that the war would end soon.

'People always think that wars will end soon. But they don't,' said Audrey. 'Why, one lasted for a hundred years. What about that?'

Monica said: 'But that was centuries ago and quite different. Nothing to do with Now.'

But Audrey wasn't at all sure that it was so very different.

'It's as if I'm twins,' she said to Monica one day in an attempt to explain herself. 'Do you ever feel like that?' But it seemed that Monica never did feel like that or if she did she didn't want to talk about it.

Yet there it was. Only one of the twins accepted. The other felt lost, betrayed, forsaken, a wanderer in a very dark wood. The other told her that all she accepted so meekly was quite mad, potty. And here even books let her down, for no book – at least no book that Audrey had ever read – even hinted at this essential wrongness or pottiness.

Only yesterday, for instance, she had come across it in *Nothing So Blue*. *Nothing So Blue* belonged to her, for she often bought books – most of them Penguins, but some from second-hand shops. She always wrote her name on the fly-leaf and tried to blot out any signs of previous ownership. But this book had been very difficult. It had taken her more than an hour to rub out the pencil marks that had been found all through it. They began harmlessly, 'Read and enjoyed by Charles Edwin Roofe in this Year of our Salvation MCMXLII, which being interpreted is Thank You Very Much', continued 'Blue?

Rather pink, I think', and, throughout the whole of the book, the word 'blue' – which of course often occurred – was underlined and in the margin there would be a question mark, a note of exclamation, or 'Ha, ha'. 'Nauseating', he had written on the page which began 'I looked her over and decided she would do'. Then came the real love affair with the beautiful English girl who smelt of daffodils and Mr Roofe had relapsed into 'Ha, ha – sez you!' But it was on page 166 that Audrey had a shock. He had written 'Women are an unspeakable abomination' with such force that the pencil had driven through the paper. She had torn the page out and thrown it into the fireplace. Fancy that! There was no fire, of course, so she was able to pick it up, smooth it out and stick it back.

'Why should I spoil my book?' she had thought. All the same she felt terribly down for some reason. And yet, she told herself, 'I bet if you met that man he would be awfully ordinary, just like everybody else.' It was something about his small, neat, precise handwriting that made her think so. But it was always the most ordinary things that suddenly turned round and showed you another face, a terrifying face. That was the hidden horror, the horror everybody pretended did not exist, the horror that was responsible for all the other horrors.

The book was not so cheering, either. It was about damp, moist heat, birds that did not sing, flowers that had no scent. Then there was this horrible girl whom the hero simply had to make love to, though he didn't really want to, and when the lovely, cool English girl heard about it she turned him down.

The natives were surly. They always seemed to be jeering behind your back. And they were stupid. They believed everything they were told, so that they could be easily worked up against somebody. Then they became cruel – so horribly cruel, you wouldn't believe . . .

And the insects. Not only the rats, snakes and poisonous spiders, scorpions, centipedes, millions of termites in their earth-coloured nests from which branched out yards of elaborately built communication lines leading sometimes to a smaller nest, sometimes to an untouched part of the tree on which they were feeding, while sometimes they just petered out, empty. It was no use poking at a nest with a stick. It seemed vulnerable, but the insects would swarm, whitely horrible, to its defence, and would rebuild it in a night. The only thing was to smoke them out. Burn them alive-oh. And even then some would escape and at once start building somewhere else.

Finally, there were the minute crawling unseen things that got at you as you walked along harmlessly. Most horrible of all these was the jigger.

Audrey stopped reading. She had a headache. Perhaps that was because she had not had anything to eat all day; unless you can count a cup of tea at eight in the morning as something to eat. But she did not often get a weekday off and when she did not a moment must be wasted. So from ten to two, regardless of sirens wailing, she went shopping in Oxford Street, and she skipped lunch. She bought stockings, a nightgown and a dress. It was buying the dress that had taken it out of her. The assistant had tried to sell her a print dress a size too big and, when she did not want it, had implied that it was unpatriotic to make so much fuss about what she wore. 'But the colours are so glaring and it doesn't fit. It's much too short,' Audrey said.

'You could easily let it down.'

Audrey said: 'But there's nothing to let down. I'd like to try on that dress over there.'

'It's a very small size.'

'Well, I'm thin enough,' said Audrey defiantly. 'How much thinner d'you want me to be?'

'But that's a dress for a girl,' the assistant said.

And suddenly, what with the pain in her back and everything, Audrey had wanted to cry. She nearly said 'I work just as hard as you,' but she was too dignified.

'The grey one looks a pretty shape,' she said. 'Not so drear. Drear,' she repeated, because that was a good word and if the assistant knew anything she would place her by it. But the woman, not at all impressed, stared over her head.

'The dresses on that rail aren't your size. You can try one on if you like but it wouldn't be any use. You could easily let down the print one,' she repeated maddeningly.

Audrey had felt like a wet rag after her defeat by the shop assistant, for she had ended by buying the print dress. It would not be enough to go and spruce up in the Ladies' Room on the fifth floor – which would be milling full of Old Things – so she had gone home again, back to the flat she shared with Monica. There had not been time to eat anything, but she had put on the new dress and it looked even worse than it had looked in the shop. From the neck to the waist it was enormous, or shapeless. The skirt, on the other hand, was very short and skimpy and two buttons came off in her hand; she had to wait and sew them on again.

It had all made her very tired. And she would be late for tea at Roberta's . . .

'I wish I lived here,' she thought when she came out of the Tube station. But she often thought that when she went to a different part of London. 'It's nicer here,' she'd think, 'I might be happier here.'

Her friend Roberta's house was painted green and had a small garden. Audrey felt envious as she pressed the bell. And still more envious when Roberta came to the door wearing a flowered house coat, led the way into a pretty sitting-room and collapsed onto her sofa in a film-star attitude. Audrey's immediate thought was 'What right has a woman got to be lolling about like that in wartime, even if she is going to have a baby?' But when she noticed Roberta's deep-circled eyes, her huge, pathetic stomach, her spoilt hands, her broken nails, and realized that her house coat had been made out of a pair of old curtains ('not half so pretty as she was. Looks much older') she said the usual things, warmly and sincerely.

But she hoped that, although it was nearly six by the silver clock, Roberta would offer her some tea and cake. Even a plain slice of bread – she could have wolfed that down.

'Why are you so late?' Roberta asked. 'I suppose you've had tea,' and hurried on before Audrey could open her mouth. 'Have a chocolate biscuit.'

So Audrey ate a biscuit slowly. She felt she did not know Roberta well enough to say 'I'm ravenous. I must have something to eat.' Besides that was the funny thing. The more ravenous you grew, the more impossible it became to say 'I'm ravenous!'

'Is that a good book?' Roberta asked.

'I brought it to read on the Tube. It isn't bad.'

Roberta flicked through the pages of *Nothing So Blue* without much interest. And she said 'English people always mix up tropical places. My dear, I met a girl the other day who thought Moscow was the capital of India! Really, I think it's dangerous to be as ignorant as that, don't you?'

Roberta often talked about 'English' people in that way. She had acquired the habit, Audrey thought, when she was out of England for two years before the war. She had lived for six months in New York. 78 Then she had been to Miami, Trinidad, Bermuda –

all those places – and no expense spared, or so she said. She had brought back all sorts of big ideas. Much too big. Gadgets for the kitchen. An extensive wardrobe. Expensive makeup. Having her hair and nails looked after every week at the hairdresser's. There was no end to it. Anyway, there was one good thing about the war. It had taken all that right off. Right off.

'Read what he says about jiggers,' Audrey said.

'My dear,' said Roberta, 'he *is* piling it on.'

'Do you mean that there aren't such things as jiggers?'

'Of course there are such things,' Roberta said, 'but they're only sand fleas. It's better not to go barefoot if you're frightened of them.'

She explained about jiggers. They had nasty ways – the man wasn't so far wrong. She talked about tropical insects for some time after that; she seemed to remember them more vividly than anything else. Then she read out bits of *Nothing So Blue*, laughing at it.

'If you must read all the time, you needn't believe everything you read.'

'I don't,' said Audrey. 'If you knew how little I really believe you'd be surprised. Perhaps he doesn't see it the way you do. It all depends on how people see things. If someone wanted to write a horrible book about London, couldn't he write a horrible book? I wish somebody would. I'd buy it.'

'You dope!' said Roberta affectionately.

When the time came to go Audrey walked back to the Tube station in a daze, and in a daze sat in the train until a jerk of the brain warned her that she had passed Leicester Square and now had to change at King's Cross. She felt very bad when she got out, as if she could flop any minute. There were so many people pushing, you got bewildered.

She tried to think about Monica, about the end of the journey, above all about food – warm, lovely food – but something had happened inside her head and she couldn't concentrate. She kept remembering the termites. Termites running along one of the covered ways that peter out and lead to nothing. When she came to the escalator she hesitated, afraid to get on it. The people clinging to the sides looked very like large insects. No, they didn't *look* like large insects: they were insects.

She got onto the escalator and stood staidly on the right-hand side. No running up for her tonight. She pressed her arm against her side and felt the book.

That started her thinking about jiggers again. Jiggers got in under your skin when you didn't know it and laid eggs inside you. Just walking along, as you might be walking along the street to a Tube station, you caught a jigger as easily as you bought a newspaper or turned on the radio. And there you were – infected – and not knowing a thing about it.

In front of her stood an elderly woman with dank hair and mean-looking clothes. It was funny how she hated women like that. It was funny how she hated most women anyway. Elderly women ought to stay at home. They oughtn't to walk about. Depressing people! Jutting out, that was what the woman was doing. Standing right in the middle, instead of in line. So that you could hardly blame the service girl, galloping up in a hurry, for giving her a good shove and saying under her breath 'Oh get out of the way!' But she must have shoved too hard for the old thing tottered. She was going to fall. Audrey's heart jumped sickeningly into her mouth as she shut her eyes. She didn't want to see what it would look like, didn't want to hear the scream.

But no scream came and when Audrey opened her eyes she saw that the old woman had astonishingly saved herself. She had only stumbled down a couple of steps and clutched the rail again. She even managed to laugh and say 'Now I know where all the beef goes to!' Her face, though, was very white. So was Audrey's. Perhaps her heart kept turning over. So did Audrey's.

Even when she got out of the Tube the nightmare was not over. On the way home she had to walk up a little street which she hated and it was getting dark now. It was one of those streets which are nearly always empty. It had been badly blitzed and Audrey was sure that it was haunted. Weeds and wild-looking flowers were growing over the skeleton houses, over the piles of rubble. There were front doorsteps which looked as though they were hanging by a thread, and near one of them lived a black cat with green eyes. She liked cats but not this one, not this one. She was sure it wasn't a cat really.

Supposing the siren went? 'If the siren goes up when I'm in this street it'll mean that it's all U.P. with me.' Supposing a man with a strange blank face and no eyebrows – like that one who got into the Ladies at the cinema the other night and stood there grinning at them and nobody knew what to do so everybody pretended he wasn't there. Perhaps he was *not* there, either – supposing a man like that were to come up softly behind her, touch her shoulder, speak to her, she wouldn't be able to struggle, she would just lie down and die of fright, so much she hated that street. And she had to walk slowly because if she ran she would give whatever it was its opportunity and it would run after her. However, even walking slowly, it came to an end at last. Just round the corner in a placid ordinary street where all the damage had been tidied up was the third floor flat which she shared with Monica, also a typist in a government office.

The radio was on full tilt. The smell of cabbage drifted down the stairs. Monica, for once, was getting the meal ready. They ate out on Mondays, Wednesdays and Fridays, in on Tuesdays, Thursdays, Saturdays and Sundays. Audrey usually did the housework and cooking and Monica took charge of the ration books, stood in long queues to shop and lugged the laundry back and forwards every week because the van didn't call any longer.

'Hullo,' said Monica.

Audrey answered her feebly, 'Hullo.'

Monica, a dark, pretty girl, put the food on the table and remarked at once, 'You're a bit green in the face. Have you been drinking mock gin?'

'Oh, don't be funny. I haven't had much to eat today – that's all.'

After a few minutes Monica said impatiently, 'Well why don't you eat then?'

'I think I've gone past it,' said Audrey, fidgeting with the sausage and cabbage on her plate.

Monica began to read from the morning paper. She spoke loudly above the music on the radio.

'Have you seen this article about being a woman in Germany? It says they can't get any scent or eau-de-cologne or nail polish.'

'Fancy that!' Audrey said. 'Poor things!'

'It says the first thing Hitler stopped was nail polish. He began that way. I wonder why. He must have had a reason, mustn't he?'

'Why must he have had a reason?' said Audrey.

'Because,' said Monica, 'if they've got a girl thinking she isn't pretty, thinking she's shabby, they've got her where they want her, as a rule. And it might start with nail polish, see? And it says: "All the old women and the middle-aged women look most terribly unhappy. They simply *slink* about," it says.'

'You surprise me,' Audrey said. 'Different in the Isle of Dogs, isn't it?'

She was fed up now and she wanted to be rude to

somebody. 'Oh *do* shut up,' she said. 'I'm not interested. Why should I have to cope with German women as well as all the women over here? What a nightmare!'

Monica opened her mouth to answer sharply; then shut it again. She was an even-tempered girl. She piled the plates onto a tray, took it into the kitchen and began to wash up.

As soon as she had gone Audrey turned off the radio and the light. Blissful sleep, lovely sleep, she never got enough of it ... On Sunday mornings, long after Monica was up, she would lie unconscious. A heavy sleeper, you might call her, except that her breathing was noiseless and shallow and that she lay so still, without tossing or turning. And then *She* (*who?*) *sent the gentle sleep from Heaven that slid into my soul. That slid into my soul. Sleep, Nature's sweet, something-or-the-other. The sleep that knits up the ravelled* ...

It seemed that she had hardly shut her eyes when she was awake again. Monica was shaking her.

'What's the matter? Is it morning?' Audrey said. 'What is it? What is it?'

'Oh, nothing at all,' Monica said sarcastically. 'You were only shrieking the place down.'

'Was I?' Audrey said, interested. 'What was I saying?'

'I don't know what you were saying and I don't care. But if you're trying to get us turned out, that's the way to do it. You know perfectly well that the woman downstairs is doing all she can to get us out because she says we are too noisy. You said something about jiggers. What *are* jiggers anyway?'

'It's slang for people in the Tube,' Audrey answered glibly to her great surprise. 'Didn't you know that?'

'Oh is it? No, I never heard that.'

'The name comes from a tropical insect,' Audrey said, 'that gets in under your skin when you don't know it. It lays eggs and hatches them out and you don't know it. And there's another sort of tropical insect that lives in enormous cities. They have railways, Tubes, bridges, soldiers, wars, everything we have. And they have big cities, and smaller cities with roads going from one to another. Most of them are what they call workers. They never fly because they've lost their wings and they never make love either. They're just workers. Nobody quite knows how this is done, but they think it's the food. Other people say it's segregation. Don't you believe me?'

she said, her voice rising. 'Do you think I'm telling lies?'

'Of course I believe you,' said Monica soothingly, 'but I don't see why you should shout about it.'

Audrey drew a deep breath. The corners of her mouth quivered. Then she said 'Look, I'm going to bed. I'm awfully tired. I'm going to take six aspirins and then go to bed. If the siren goes don't wake me up. Even if one of those things seems to be coming very close, don't wake me up. I don't want to be woken up whatever happens.'

'Very well,' Monica said. 'All right, old girl.'

Audrey rushed at her with clenched fists and began to shriek again. 'Damn you, don't call me that. Damn your soul to everlasting hell *don't call me that* . . .'

PENGUIN 60s

MARTIN AMIS · *God's Dice*

HANS CHRISTIAN ANDERSEN · *The Emperor's New Clothes*

MARCUS AURELIUS · *Meditations*

JAMES BALDWIN · *Sonny's Blues*

AMBROSE BIERCE · *An Occurrence at Owl Creek Bridge*

DIRK BOGARDE · *From Le Pigeonnier*

WILLIAM BOYD · *Killing Lizards*

POPPY Z. BRITE · *His Mouth will Taste of Wormwood*

ITALO CALVINO · *Ten Italian Folktales*

ALBERT CAMUS · *Summer*

TRUMAN CAPOTE · *First and Last*

RAYMOND CHANDLER · *Goldfish*

ANTON CHEKHOV · *The Black Monk*

ROALD DAHL · *Lamb to the Slaughter*

ELIZABETH DAVID · *I'll be with You in the Squeezing of a Lemon*

N. J. DAWOOD (TRANS.) · *The Seven Voyages of Sindbad the Sailor*

ISAK DINESEN · *The Dreaming Child*

SIR ARTHUR CONAN DOYLE · *The Man with the Twisted Lip*

DICK FRANCIS · *Racing Classics*

SIGMUND FREUD · *Five Lectures on Psycho-Analysis*

KAHLIL GIBRAN · *Prophet, Madman, Wanderer*

STEPHEN JAY GOULD · *Adam's Navel*

ALASDAIR GRAY · *Five Letters from an Eastern Empire*

GRAHAM GREENE · *Under the Garden*

JAMES HERRIOT · *Seven Yorkshire Tales*

PATRICIA HIGHSMITH · *Little Tales of Misogyny*

M. R. JAMES AND R. L. STEVENSON · *The Haunted Dolls' House*

RUDYARD KIPLING · *Baa Baa, Black Sheep*

PENELOPE LIVELY · *A Long Night at Abu Simbel*

KATHERINE MANSFIELD · *The Escape*

PENGUIN 60s